OLIVER JEFFERS

The Heart and the BOTTLE

HarperCollins *Children's Books*

For Gerard

First published in hardback in Great Britain by HarperCollins Children's Books in 2010

1 3 5 7 9 10 8 6 4 2

ISBN: 978-0-00-718230-5

HarperCollins Children's Books is a division of HarperCollins Publishers Ltd.

Text and illustrations copyright © Oliver Jeffers 2010

Art Assistance: Robbii Albright
Additional artwork by Frieda Premo on page 12

Visit our website at: www.harpercollins.co.uk

Printed in China

Once there was a girl, much like any other,

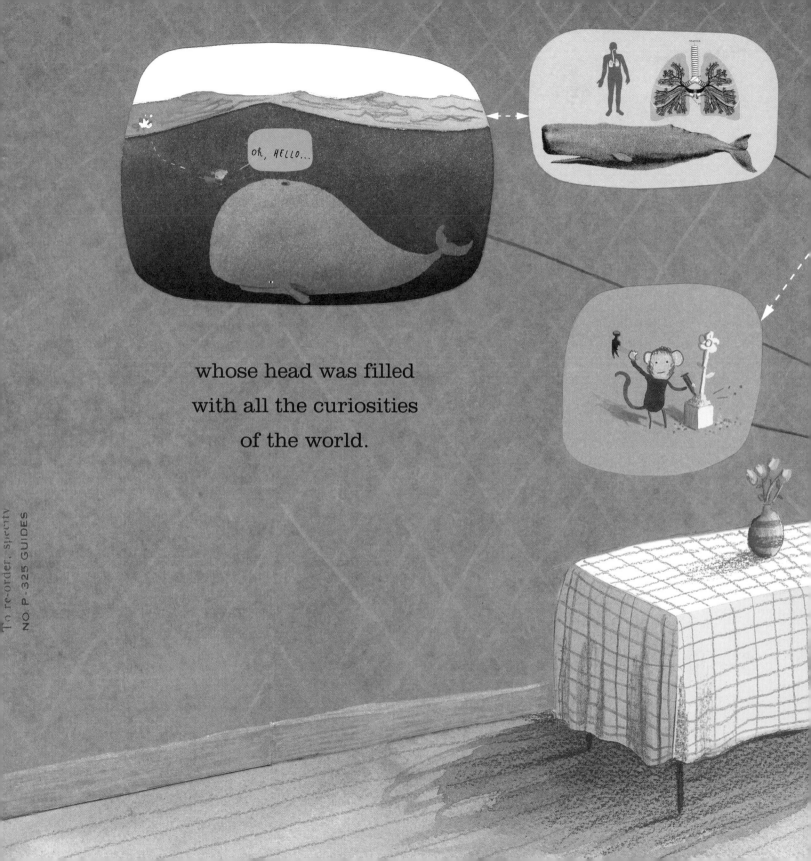

whose head was filled
with all the curiosities
of the world.

With thoughts of the stars.

With wonder at the sea.

She took delight in finding new things...

...until the day she found an empty chair.

Feeling unsure, the girl thought the best thing was to put her heart in a safe place.

Just for the time being.

So, she put it in a bottle and hung it around her neck...

and that seemed to fix things...

at first.

Although in truth, nothing was the same.

She forgot about the stars...

and stopped taking notice of the sea.

She was no longer filled
with all the curiosities of the
world and didn't take much
notice of anything…

other than
how heavy…

and awkward
the bottle
had become.

But at least her
heart was safe.

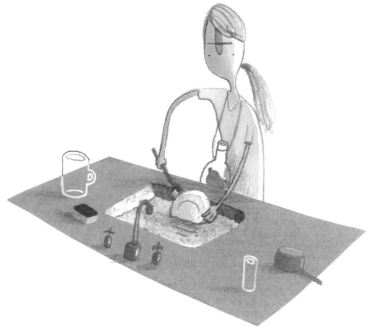

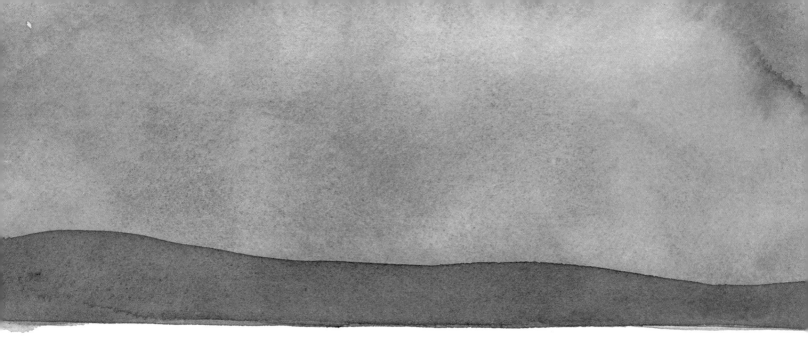

It might never have
occurred to the girl what to
do had she not met someone
smaller and still curious
about the world.

There was a time
when the girl would have
known how to answer her.

But not now.

Not without her heart.

And it was right
at that moment
she decided to get it
back out of the bottle.

But didn't know how.

She couldn't remember.

And nothing seemed to work.

The bottle couldn't be broken.

It just bounced and rolled...

right down to the sea.

But there, it occurred to
someone smaller and still
curious about the world that she
might know a way.

And it just so happened…

she did.

The heart was put back where it came from.

And the chair wasn't so empty any more.

But the bottle was.

AORTIC
ARCH

SUPERIOR
Vena CAVA

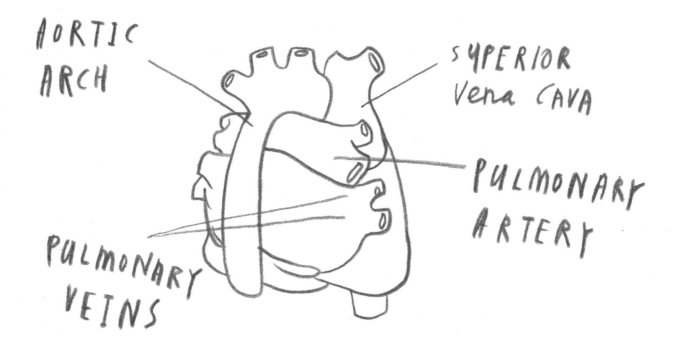

PULMONARY
ARTERY

PULMONARY
VEINS

the
HEART
AND VESSELS
(posterior view)